Treasure

Suzanne Bloom

BOYDS MILLS PRESS

HONESDALE, PENNSYLVANIA

Boyds Mills Press, Inc.
815 Church Street
Honesdale, Pennsylvania 18431
Printed in China

Library of Congress Cataloging-in-Publication Data

Bloom, Suzanne.
  Treasure / Suzanne Bloom.—1st ed.
       p. cm.
  Summary: When Bear follows Goose on what he thinks is a treasure hunt,
they make a wonderful discovery.
  ISBN 978-1-59078-457-0 (hardcover : alk. paper)
  [1. Treasure hunt (Game)—Fiction. 2. Friendship—Fiction. 3. Bears—Fiction.
  4. Geese—Fiction.] I. Title.

  PZ7.B6234Tre 2007
  [E]—dc22
                                        2006037946

First edition
The text of this book is set in 42-point Optima.
The illustrations are done in pastel.

10 9 8 7 6 5 4 3 2 1

4158

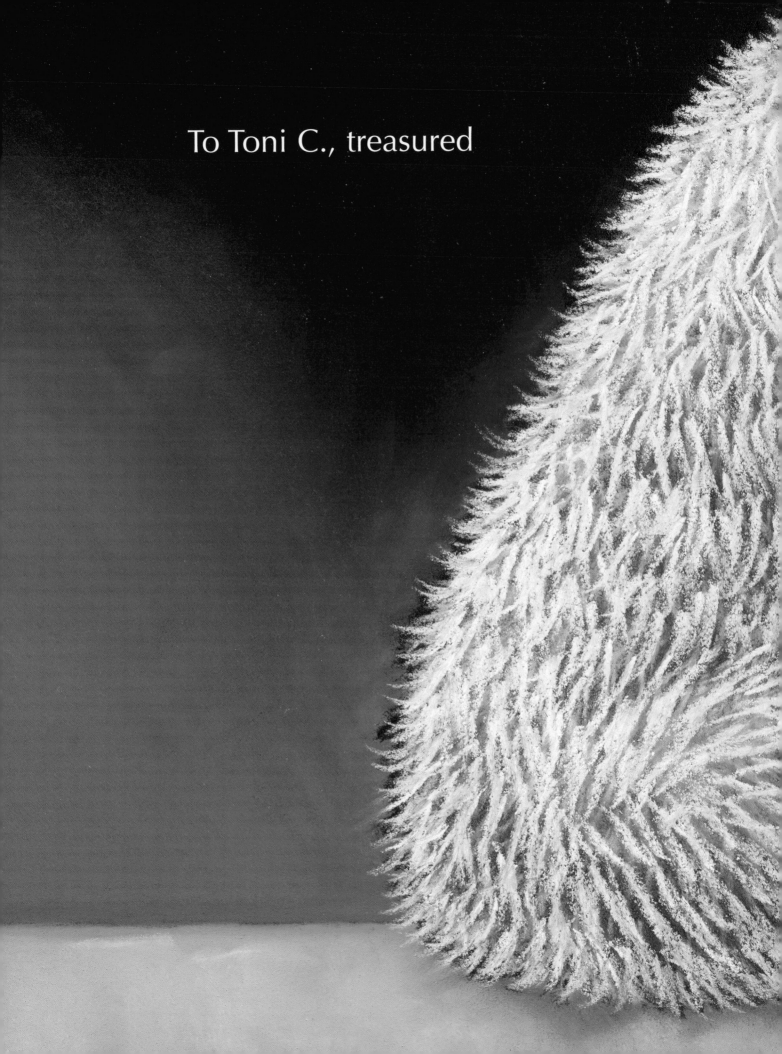

To Toni C., treasured

What are you doing?

Are you looking
for treasure?

I like to look for treasure.
Yo ho ho!

Wait right here.
I'll get my gear.

I'm back.
I'm packed.
Let's go!

Are we there yet?
Let's look.

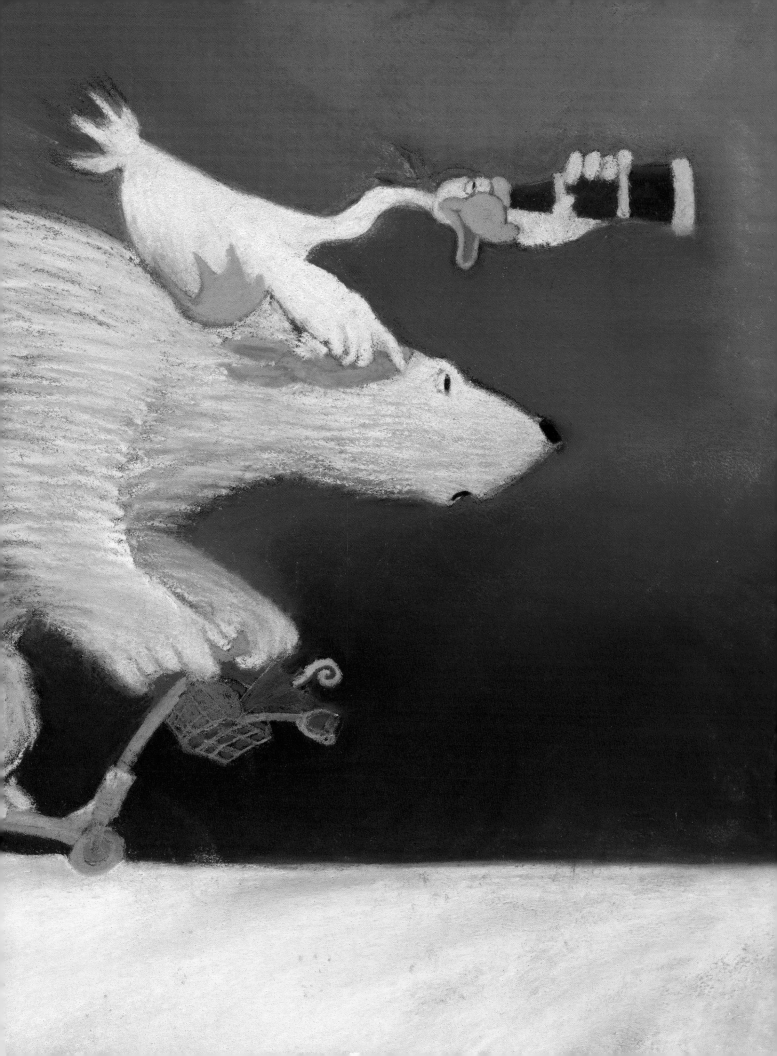

Is it buried treasure?
Let's dig.

Is it sunken treasure?
Let's dive.

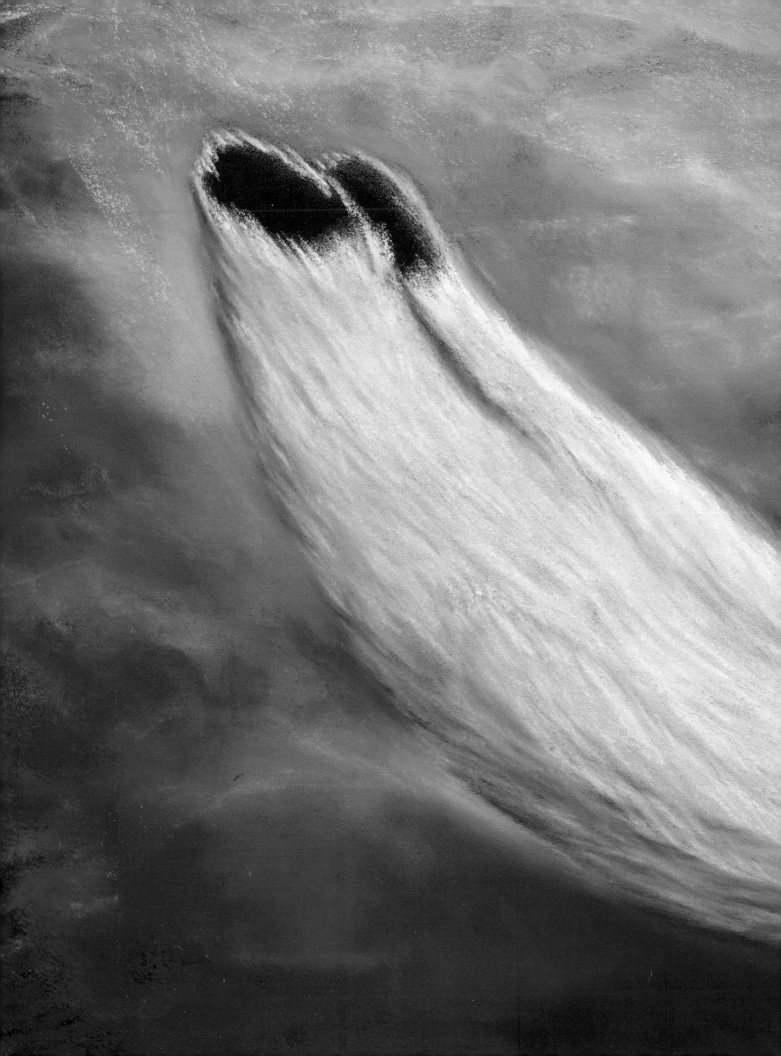

There is no treasure.
We didn't find
any treasure at all.

Yes we did.
We had a splendid day . . .

and you are a treasure.

I am a treasure?

Yes, indeed.
You are my treasure.
Yo ho ho!

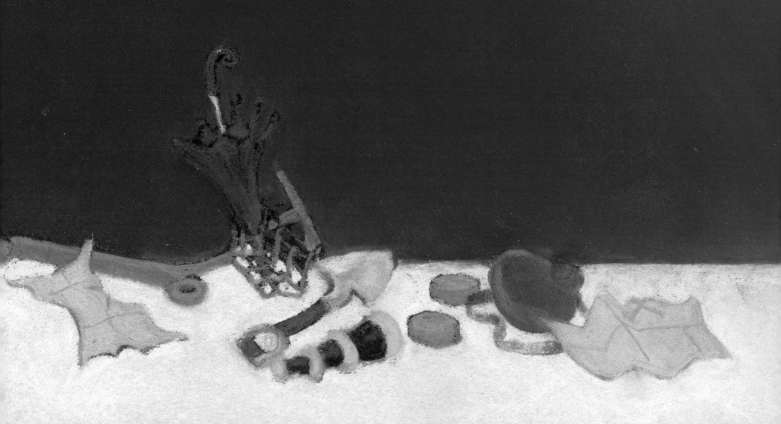

Oh! Yes!
You are my treasure, too.
Yo ho ho, indeed!

MAR   2008